Bike Daredevils

Felice Arena and Phil Kettle

CRIEFF PRIMARY SCHOOL
COMMISSIONER STREET
CRIEFF

illustrated by
David Cox

RISING★STARS

First published in Great Britain by
RISING STARS UK LTD 2004
22 Grafton Street, London, W1S 4EX

Reprinted 2004, 2005, 2006, 2007

All rights reserved.

No part of this publication may be produced, stored in a retrieval system,
or transmitted, in any form by any means, electronic, mechanical,
photocopying, recording or otherwise, without the prior permission of the
copyright owner.

For information visit our website at:
www.risingstars-uk.com

British Library Cataloguing in Publication Data

A CIP record for this book is available from the British Library.

ISBN: 978-1-904591-72-6

First published in 2003 by
MACMILLAN EDUCATION AUSTRALIA PTY LTD
627 Chapel Street, South Yarra, Australia 3141

Associated companies and representatives throughout the world.

Visit our website at www.macmillan.com.au or
go directly to www.macmillanlibrary. com.au.

Copyright © Felice Arena and Phil Kettle 2003

Project Management by Limelight Press Pty Ltd
Cover and text design by Lore Foye
Illustrations by David Cox

Printed in China

Contents

Josh   Con

CHAPTER 1

A Balancing Act

In a quiet suburban street, best friends Josh and Con are casually riding their bikes around in circles on the grass in front of Con's house.

Josh "What gear are you in?"

Con "Fourth. You?"

Josh "First. Can you balance on the spot without pedalling?"

Con "Yeah. Can you?"

Josh "Yeah, 'course!"

Con "How long can you do it for?"

Josh "Don't know—probably about two minutes."

Con "No way! That's pretty long."

Josh "No it's not. Look, I'll show you! You time me."

Con "I haven't got a watch."

Josh "Me neither. Just time me by saying 'one Mississippi, two Mississippi' ..."

Con "What?"

Josh "When you say 'one
Mississippi', it's about one second."

Con "Oh, like 'one monkey-kneebone,
two monkey-kneebone' ..."

Josh "Yeah—like that."

Con "Okay. One Mississippi, two
Missi ..."

Josh "Not yet! Wait! Start counting
when I say I'm ready."

Josh stops pedalling his bike and gently squeezes his brakes until he rolls to a standstill. He stands up out of his seat, swaying from side to side, struggling to keep upright.

Josh "Now!"

Con "One Mississippi, two
Mississippi, three Mississippi,
four monkey-kneebone, five
monkey-kneebone ..."

Josh suddenly loses his balance
and begins to fall.

CHAPTER 2

And for My Next Trick ...

Josh sticks out his foot and slams it down on the ground, stopping himself and his bike from completely toppling over.

Con "That was only five seconds!"

Josh "You put me off by changing to 'monkey-kneebone'!"

Con "So?"

Josh "So—I like 'Mississippi'!"

Con "It shouldn't make any difference—I'm the one counting."

Josh "Yeah, well, it put me off. Let me do it again. But this time let's pick a counting word we both like."

Con "Okay. What about 'one lumpy-custard, two lumpy-custard' ...?"

Josh "Or, I know ... 'one snotty-nose, two snotty-nose' ...!"

Josh and Con snort and chuckle at each other, proud of their made-up, time-keeping words.

Con "Forget balancing. I've got a better idea. Let's jump over a ramp!"

Josh "Yeah! Wicked! But what ramp?"

Con "We'll make one. Come on."

The boys hop off their bikes and charge around to Con's back garden. They return with a plank of wood and a couple of bricks. They make their ramp—placing one end of the wood on top of the two bricks.

Con "OK. I'll go first."

Con stands up out of his bike seat and frantically crunches down on his pedals. He sprints towards the ramp as if he's an Olympic cyclist racing for the finishing line.

CHAPTER 3

Daredevils

Con makes it! He jumps off the ramp
and rides back to Josh.

Con "Did you see that? It was unreal! I felt like I was flying. I got about a metre off the ground."

Josh "No you didn't. It was only a few centimetres."

Con "No way! It was higher than that."

Josh "In your dreams. My turn. Here goes! … *Ladies, gentlemen and thrill-seekers, here comes the greatest stuntman in the world … the Amazing Josh!*"

Con "You're going to jump a ramp, not make a rabbit disappear!"

Josh "Okay, then what should I call myself?"

Con "Nothing. Just jump!"

Josh "No, I have to have a name— like Evel Knievel!"

Con "Who?"

Josh "Evel Knievel! He was a
famous daredevil motorbike rider
when my dad was young. He used
to jump over cars and stuff."

Con "Cool!"

Josh "So maybe I could be 'Evel
Josh' ... nah, 'Jumping Josh' ... or
'Jumping Josh Flash' ..."

Con "How about 'Hurry Up Josh'?"

Josh "I've got it! 'Jumping Josh
Warrior'!"

Con "That's it?"

Josh "Yeah! ... *And a sudden hush sweeps across the crowd as Jumping Josh Warrior prepares to take the leap of his life. Will he make it safely to the other side? No-one has ever attempted to jump over the Blackpool Tower before. This is going to be incredible ... and here he goes.*"

Josh rushes towards the ramp and sails over it easily. Con jumps again, then so does Josh. Both boys continue to ride over the ramp for several minutes.

Con "This is boring. We've got to jump over something that's real. I know what!"

CHAPTER 4

Leap of Faith

Con rides his bike over to the side
fence. Josh wonders what Con has
in mind.

Josh "What are we going to jump
over?"

Con "You'll see. Chico! Here Chico!"

Suddenly, an excited, little, white, fluffy dog appears from nowhere and runs to Con.

Josh "You're not seriously going to jump over a dog?"

Con "Well, it's not *my* dog—it's from next door."

Josh "But what if you miss?"

Con "I won't! Look how small he is."

Josh "Well I don't think *I* can jump over him."

Con "But you're the amazing Jumping Josh Warrior!"

Con hops off his bike and picks up Chico. He takes the dog and places it only a few centimetres away from the other side of the ramp.

Con "Stay Chico! Don't move. That's
a good boy. Stay!"

Con runs back to Josh and hops
on his bike, ready to jump over his
neighbour's dog.

Josh "Poor little fella."

Con "He's going to be okay! Just you wait and see. This is going to be awesome—better than jumping over some fake tower.

... And there's another hush from the crowd. They loved Jumping Josh Warrior, but now it's Captain Courageous Con's turn."

Josh "You mean, Captain *Crazy* Con!"

Con suddenly pedals as fast as he can towards the ramp, while Chico wags his tail, unaware of what is about to happen to him.

CHAPTER 5

Oh No!

As the front tyre of Con's bike makes contact with the ramp, Josh suddenly yells out.

Josh "Chico! Chico! Here boy!"

Chico jumps up and scampers
over to Josh, just as Con tries to
leap over the top of him. Josh lets
out a huge sigh of relief and picks
Chico up.

Con "What do you think you're
doing? I would've made it!"

Josh "No, you wouldn't. Look! Your
back wheel hit the ground just
where Chico's head would've been."

Con "Really?"

Josh "Yeah—Chico would've ended
up being a Chico Roll!"

Con "Phew! That was lucky."

Josh "Is there anything else we can
jump over?"

Con "Um ... Wait, I know!"

Con hops off his bike and runs
into his house. He returns clutching
an armful of dolls.

Josh "Dolls?"

Con "Yeah, my sister's dumb dolls.
We'll line them all up. And who
cares if we miss and land on them.
Right?"

Josh "Cool!"

As Con and Josh prepare to leap
over the dolls, Con's sister suddenly
appears and yells, "Con!! Don't you
dare or I'm telling Mum!!"

Con "You ready to go for it, Jumping Josh Warrior?"

Josh "You bet, Captain Courageous Con!"

Both boys rush towards the ramp.
"MUM!!!!!!!!!!" screams Con's sister.

axle The metal rod between the wheels that helps them to turn.

bike pump A tool used to pump up a flat tyre.

helmet Protects your head if you happen to fall off your bike.

pedals What you put your feet on to push the bike.

puncture A hole your bike tyre gets that makes the tyre go flat.

BOYS RULE!
Bike Must-dos

☞ Make sure you always put your helmet on before you ride your bike.

☞ Remember to check the air pressure in your tyres.

☞ If you ride through puddles, make sure you wash the mud off your clothes before you go home.

☞ Learn how to mend punctures.

☞ Make sure that you know the highway code before you ride in the streets.

☞ If you want your bike to go faster, cut strips of cardboard and peg them to your wheel rims—the more wind you create in your spokes the more noise your bike will make and the faster it will go.

☞ Always wear shoes. If your feet hit the ground and you haven't got shoes on, you might not have any feet left.

☞ If you're riding on a path in a park, make sure you ring your bell when you see someone on the path.

☞ The most important bike rule is: look left, look right, then go ahead with extreme care.

Bike Instant Info

 The first pedal power pushbike was made in 1865. It was so rough that it was known as "the boneshaker".

 The first pushbike with solid rubber wheels was made in 1870. This was also the first bike to be called a bicycle.

In 1898 the first bike, that looks something like the bike that you ride today, was built.

The first bike race took place in 1868, over a distance of 1200 metres.

BMX racing first started in California in 1969.

 The most famous bike race in the world is the Tour de France.

 The highest bicycle bunny hop cleared a vertical bar of 116 centimetres.

 The fastest bicycle speed ever recorded is 268.8 kilometres per hour. The bike was travelling behind a windshield.

 The longest bicycle ever built was 25.9 metres.

 The best bicycle in the world is the one that you own.

BOYS RULE!
Think Tank

1 How do you make your bike go faster?

2 What side of the road do you ride on in Great Britain?

3 What side of the road do you ride on in America?

4 What do you call a bike that has three wheels?

5 What is a tandem bike?

6 What is the most famous bike race in the world?

7 Who is the best person in the world to mend a puncture on your bike?

8 Should you always wear a helmet when you ride your bike?

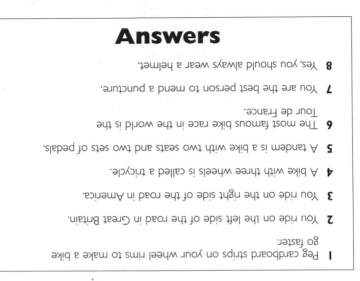

Answers

1 Peg cardboard strips on your wheel rims to make a bike go faster.

2 You ride on the left side of the road in Great Britain.

3 You ride on the right side of the road in America.

4 A bike with three wheels is called a tricycle.

5 A tandem is a bike with two seats and two sets of pedals.

6 The most famous bike race in the world is the Tour de France.

7 You are the best person to mend a puncture.

8 Yes, you should always wear a helmet.

How did you score?

- If you got 8 correct answers, then put on your bike helmet and go for a ride.

- If you got only 6 answers correct, maybe you should only ride in the park.

- If you didn't get more than 4 answers correct, either keep practising or make sure you have a good pair of shoes for walking.

Felice → ← Phil

Hi Guys!

We have loads of fun reading and want you to, too. We both believe that being a good reader is really important and so cool.

Try out our suggestions to help you have fun as you read.

At school, why don't you use "Bike Daredevils" as a play and you and your best friend can be the actors. Set the scene for your play. What props do you need? Maybe a bike helmet, or just use your imagination to pretend that you are at the park and about to have a bike race with your friends.

So ... have you decided who is going to be Josh and who is going to be Con? Now, with your friends, read and act out our story in front of the class.

We have a lot of fun when we go to schools and read our stories. After we finish the kids all clap really loudly. When you've finished your play your classmates will do the same. Just remember to look out of the window— there might be a talent scout from a television station watching you!

Reading at home is really important and a lot of fun as well.

Take our books home and get someone in your family to read them with you. Maybe they can take on a part in the story.

Remember, reading is a whole lot of fun.

So, as the frog in the local pond would say, Read-it!

And remember, Boys Rule!

BOYS RULE!
When We Were Kids

Felice *Phil*

Phil "How did you make your bike go faster when you were a kid, Felice?"

Felice "I'd peg cardboard flaps to the rims of my back wheel."

Phil "And did that make you go faster?"

Felice "Well, you have heard about cars with big exhaust pipes?"

Phil "Yeah."

Felice "The louder the noise, the faster the car goes. The same went for my bike … still does."

Phil "So did that work?"

Felice "Yep, most of the time. But if that failed, I'd use my mouth, as I pedalled, to go *vrrrrrooooom*!"

BOYS RULE!

What a Laugh!

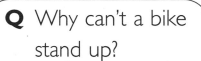

Q Why can't a bike stand up?

A Because it's two-tyred.

BOYS RULE!

Gone Fishing

The Tree House

Golf Legends

Camping Out

Bike Daredevils

Water Rats

Skateboard
Dudes

Tennis Ace

Basketball
Buddies

Secret Agent
Heroes

Wet World

Rock Star

Pirate Attack

Olympic
Champions

Race Car
Dreamers

Hit the Beach

Rotten
School Day

Halloween
Gotcha!

Battle of the
Games

On the Farm

44

BOYS RULE! books are available from most booksellers.
For mail order information please call Rising Stars
on 0870 40 20 40 8 or visit www.risingstars-uk.com